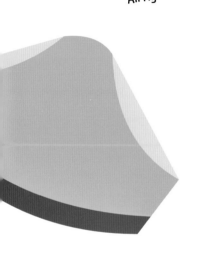

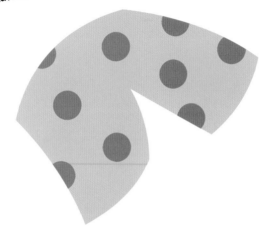

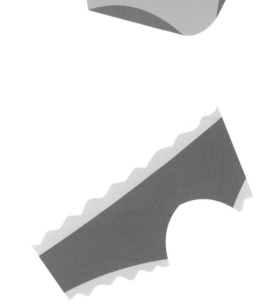

Published in the United States in 2010 by
🍎 Blue Apple Books , 515 Valley Street,
Maplewood, N.J. 07040
www.blueapplebooks.com

First Edition   Printed in China
ISBN: 978-1-60905-016-0
10 9 8 7 6 5 4 3 2

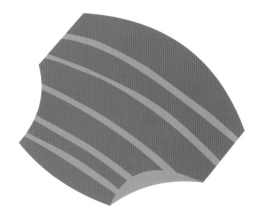

Distributed in the U.S. by Chronicle Books

Bear in Underwear

Todd H. Doodler

🍎 BLUE APPLE BOOKS

Cougar hid.

Porcupine hid.

Big Foot hid.

Turtle hid.

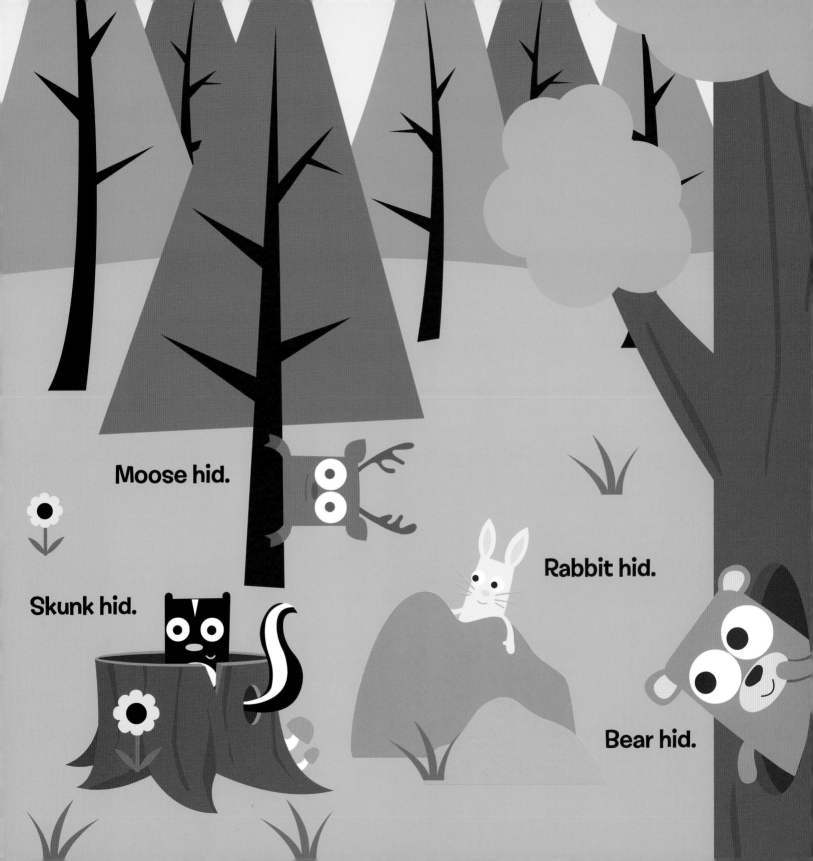

Moose hid.

Skunk hid.

Rabbit hid.

Bear hid.

Bear waited and waited.

When no one came to find him,
he decided to head home.

As Bear
jogged,
he thought of
hamburgers,
hot dogs . . .

cupcakes,
cookies,
and
ice cream.

Bear put on
a pair of
blue underwear.

He tried on another pair.

TOO LOOSE.

WHOOPS.

Bear tried on everything from the backpack.

Bear was ready to give up.
But there was
one more pair left.

Bear held up the underwear.

He put his right leg in, then his left.

He pulled and tugged.

Bear stood there with a smile wide and bright.

Bear in underwear looked

DY-NO-MITE!

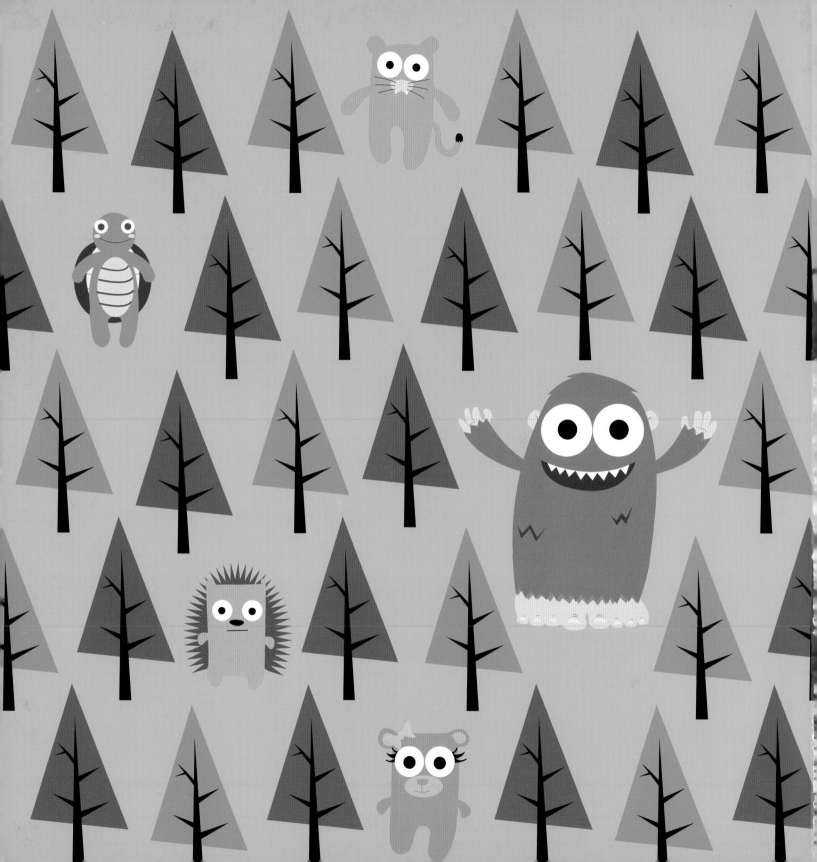